KNUT AND FREYA IN WALES

Written and Illustrated by

Mary Arrigan

POOLBEG
FOR CHILDREN

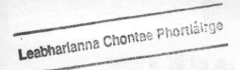
Published by
Poolbeg Press Ltd
123 Baldoyle Industrial Estate
Dublin 13, Ireland
E-mail: poolbeg@poolbeg.com
www.poolbeg.com

© Mary Arrigan 2000

Copyright for typesetting, layout, design
© Poolbeg Press Ltd

The moral right of the author has been asserted.

A catalogue record for this book is available from the British Library.

ISBN 1 85371 914 5

Cover design by Artmark
Illustrations by Mary Arrigan
Printed by The Guernsey Press Ltd,
Vale, Guernsey, Channel Islands.

KNUT
AND
FREYA
IN WALES

About the author

Award-winning author Mary Arrigan
has written many books for teenagers
as well as writing and illustrating
books for younger readers. She
taught art for eighteen years before
becoming a full-time writer. Mary,
who has two grown-up sons and a
daughter, lives beside an old abbey
near Roscrea in Co Tipperary.

For Snaffles,
my faithful friend.

Chapter One

Freya was Knut's very best friend. She lived with her Da, Sven the Blacksmith, in a small hut near Knut's longhouse. Knut's Da was a Viking chieftain called Siggy the Big and his Ma was called Helga the Huge.

Knut's hobby was carving bowls. He liked nothing better than to sit down with a chunk of wood and turn it into a soup bowl if it was small, or a bath if it was big. There wasn't much call for the bath bowls because the Vikings weren't really into that kind of thing.

"I worry about you, son," sighed Helga the Huge. "Hammering bowls is a poncy thing for a Viking."

"Huh!" snorted Knut. "I'm not hammering, Ma. I'm carving. There's a difference. Do you think it would be a nice surprise for Da if I carved a bath for when he comes back from his raid?"

"Ha!" laughed Helga the Huge.

"When your Da gets back from a raid all he ever wants to do is put his smelly feet up and drink the sour wine that he steals from foreigners."

Knut's Da did quite a lot of raiding with his band of hairy warriors. They sailed on a longship to distant countries where they nicked other people's stuff – mostly sour wine and stinky leather. Helga the Huge and all the other Viking women were pretty fed up with sour wine and stinky leather, but at least such raids kept the hairy warriors busy and stopped them fighting among themselves and messing up the place.

One sunny morning, just after the farm rooster screeched a new day, four strangers wandered into the Viking village. This caused a great fuss because people hardly ever wandered into a Viking village unless they'd been tied up and dragged in as prisoners. Helga the Huge put her hands on her hips and frowned. As the wife of the chieftain it was up to her whether to tie up these cheeky visitors or be polite.

"Be polite, Ma," said Knut. "They look harmless. Who knows, maybe they'll buy a bowl or two as souvenirs."

So Helga the Huge invited the four travellers into the longhouse and offered them some sour wine from the last raid. The travellers smelled the wine.

"Have you got a problem with our good wine?" asked Helga the Huge, crossing her big arms across her big chest. It was one thing for the Viking women to sneer at the wine their menfolk brought back, but it was quite another to have strangers sniffing it and making faces.

"N-n-no, Missus," said the tallest traveller, with a funny accent. "It's just that we're more used to leek soup ourselves. Being Welsh, you see."

Knut sat in the corner, carving away as he watched the four strangers nervously gulping the sour wine under Helga's ferocious gaze.

"You lot just passing through?" she asked.

The four men looked at one another.

"Er, yes, Missus," said the tallest one. "We're - eh - on a walking tour."

"Yes, yes, a walking tour," added the others.

"So we'd best be getting along then," went on the tallest man, getting

up and wiping his mouth. "We've –
eh – a long way to go on our walking
tour."

"Long way," echoed the others,
getting up too.

Helga the Huge was disappointed.
She wanted to ask these people loads
of questions.

"Perhaps we should lock them up
until your Da gets back," she
whispered to Knut. "Maybe squeeze
a bit of news out of them."

Knut shook his head. "Let them
go, Ma. It's the polite thing to do."

So Knut and his Ma stood at the
door of the longhouse and watched
the visitors slink away.

"Rum lot, those foreigners," said

Helga the Huge. "Waste of good wine because they hadn't any news at all. Wimps."

It was much later that night when Freya came running to the longhouse.

"Knut!" she cried. "Help!"

At the sound of her frightened voice, Knut and his Ma and the rest of the villagers gathered around.

"What is it, Freya?" asked Knut. "What's wrong?"

"It's my Da," sobbed Freya. "Four men with funny accents have stolen my Da!"

Chapter Two

"They've taken Sven the Blacksmith!" exclaimed the horrified women. "It must have been those four wimpy foreigners."

"This is a right howdy-do," said Helga the Huge. "There will be a row when Siggy the Big comes home and there's no blacksmith. We'll all be blamed."

"No," said Bertha the Bootmaker. "Not us, Helga the Huge. *You* will be blamed. After all, you invited those strangers into the longhouse."

"Yes," agreed the other women. "It's your fault, Huge Helga."

At first Helga the Huge looked extremely angry, and the other women shrank back towards the door. But then she looked at Knut. "It's your fault, Knut," she said, pointing at her son.

"Me?" said Knut. "What did I do?"

"You told me to be polite to those four crooks," said Helga the Huge.

"It's your fault. It all comes of carving those stupid bowls. You should have been thumping those men about, like we normally do with people who wander in."

"What will we do without our blacksmith?" said the women. "No weapons, no helmets, no pots and pans."

"What will I do without my Da?" asked Freya, in a very small voice.

"Maybe he's just gone for a walk," suggested Knut. "You know that Sven does that all the time."

Which was quite true. Sven did an awful lot of thinking when he wasn't hammering metal things. He often wandered up the side of the mountain beside the village to think about poetic stuff like birds and mountain streams and clouds and yellow daffs.

"Why didn't he thump them?" asked Helga the Huge. "They were just four skinny little things. I'd have thumped them myself with one hand tied behind my back – if I'd been let," she added, glaring at Knut.

"Did they knock him out?" asked Bertha the Bootmaker. "Tie him up, perhaps, while he slept?"

"No. They talked," replied Freya.

"They talked?"

"Yes," continued Freya. "They talked to him about poetry. They talked about birds and mountain streams and clouds and yellow daffs."

"That's the trouble with your Da, Freya honey," put in Helga the Huge. "He thinks too much. I always said that kind of thing would land him in trouble."

"Why would anyone want to take Sven the Blacksmith?" someone asked.

"Because," replied Freya, with her hands on her hips, "my Da is the finest blacksmith in the world."

"True," agreed Helga the Huge. "Nobody knows more about metal stuff than our Sven."

"But where did they take him?" asked Bertha the Bootmaker.

"Don't know," said Freya. "Last I saw of them they were all spouting poetry as they set sail across the sea."

"Mad," said Astrid the Awkward. "Totally mad."

"Welsh," said Helga the Huge. "They said they were Welsh."

"Where do Welsh people come from?" asked Bertha the Bootmaker.

"Wales, I think," said Knut. He had once gone on a raid with his Da to Ireland, so he knew. "It's just across from Ireland."

All eyes turned to Knut. He shifted from one foot to the other, quite uncomfortable under the gaze of all the Viking women.

"Fat lot of good that's going to do us," said Helga the Huge. "We're in severe trouble. When Siggy the Big and the rest of the hairy raiders come home there will be a mighty fuss because four skinny Welsh persons stole Sven the Blacksmith. It's your fault, Knut."

Chapter Three

When all the Viking women went home, and Helga the Huge went back to bed, Freya sat in misery at the dying fire. Knut paced up and down the longhouse, feeling very bad.

"I feel very bad, Freya," he said. "If I hadn't told Ma to be polite to those strangers they'd be tied up now and your Da would still be here."

"Don't feel so bad, Knut," said Freya. "Maybe Da will make them turn back when they run out of poems."

But they both knew that was not likely to happen. Not when Sven was with people who recited poems about birds and mountain streams and clouds and yellow daffs. He was a sucker when it came to brainy stuff like that. A big tear dripped down Freya's nose and splashed onto the hearth.

"That's it," said Knut, stopping before her. "I'm going after those crooks to get your Da back, Freya.

No, don't try to stop me," he went on as Freya got up.

"Stop you?" she said. "No way. I'm coming with you."

"You can't come with me," said Knut. "It's too dangerous."

"Excuse me?" said Freya. "You think I'm going to sit here snivelling while you sail off on your own? Dream on, Knut! Sven is my Da and I'm coming whether you like it or not."

Knut knew there was no point in arguing with Freya. He had tried it once. Only once. Together they rounded up some furry blankets, a barrel of water, a big hunk of smelly cheese, some gritty bread and rubbery meat.

"Mustn't forget my chisel," said Knut, putting the precious tool he used for carving bowls inside his belt. "Never know when it might come in useful."

And so, very quietly so as not to waken the slumbering village, they loaded everything on board the small fishing boat that was moored on the beach. Soon, in the moonlight, Knut and Freya were just specks on the horizon. Up and down, up and down went the little boat on the big waves.

"Have some rubbery meat, Knut," said Freya, offering him a wobbly chunk.

"No, ta," said Knut, turning white.

"How about a bit of nice gritty

bread then?" said Freya.

"No, ta," said Knut, turning a pale shade of green.

"Some smelly cheese then?" said Freya.

"Ugh!" said Knut, now bright green, as he leaned over the side of the up-and-down boat.

"Suit yourself," said Freya, tucking into an early breakfast.

On they sailed for several days and nights, following the star that Knut remembered from the time he had gone on a raid to Ireland with his Da.

One morning, just as the last few drops of water were slopping in the barrel and the last piece of smelly

cheese was even smellier, Knut let
out a cry.

"Land, Freya! Look, there's land."

Sure enough, popping up over the
horizon was a whole bunch of
mountains. Freya gasped. She had
never seen any land other than her

own village.

"Well, I never!" she exclaimed. "So this is the rest of the world!"

As they sailed nearer, the mountains got bigger and bigger.

"Is this it?" asked Freya. "Is this Wales?"

"I don't know," admitted Knut. "All these foreign places look the same to me."

"Let's ask that man who's chasing goats down the mountain," said Freya.

Knut set the boat on course towards the foot of the mountain Freya was pointing to. The goat man stopped when he saw them. He had long red hair, a red beard and a skirt with squares on it.

"Excuse me, mister," shouted Freya. "Are we right for Wales?"

"Noo," replied the man. "Left."

"Excuse me?" said Freya.

"Left, lassie," said the man. "Och aye. Left for Wales. Just keep yon wee boat left and you'll be in Wales afore ye know it."

"But how will we know we've reached it?" asked Knut.

"Och," laughed the man. "You'll hear it."

"Hear it?" said Knut, wondering how one could hear a country.

"Aye," said the man in the skirt. "Believe me, you'll hear it. Wales! Daft lot."

"Ta very much, mister," said Freya. "Nice skirt."

Following the directions, Knut and Freya sailed along the coast, keeping the land on their left. By now there was no food left and no water.

"If we don't find Wales soon we'll starve to death and my Da will never be rescued," groaned Freya.

"Trust me, Freya," said Knut bravely. But he hadn't a clue where they were going.

"You haven't a clue where we're going, have you, Knut?" said Freya.

Knut was just about to agree with her when they heard the first sound of Wales.

"Singing," said Freya. "Sounds

like a whole gang of people singing."

"Of course," said Knut. "I told you to trust me. We've reached Wales. Now all we have to do is find your Da."

Chapter Four

Freya helped Knut to moor the small boat and tie it to a tree. Then they set off between two mountains. The drizzly rain soaked through their clothes and their boots. By now Knut was beginning to wish that he'd listened to his Ma.

"I should have let Ma tie up those

rotten blokes," he said. "Then Sven would still be at home thinking about poetry and hammering metal things and we wouldn't be here in this damp place."

"Hush, Knut," said Freya. "At least it got us out and about to see a bit of the world. We'll find my Da, you'll see."

But Knut was having doubts. There were lots of mountains and valleys in this Wales. He was beginning to wonder if they'd ever find the place where the singing was coming from. They seemed to be travelling miles and miles, yet getting nowhere.

Suddenly, from a clump of trees, a

skinny boy with a stick jumped in front of them.

"Where are you going to, boyo?" he said in a sing-song voice.

Knut and Freya stopped with surprise.

"Who are you?" asked Freya. "And what do you mean by jumping out at unsuspecting people like that? We could have died of fright right here."

"You could?" said the boy. "That's great news indeed. Everyone says I wouldn't frighten a mouse. Wow, wait till I tell them I frightened two strangers to death!"

"Well, we're not exactly dead, you know," said Knut.

"Aren't you even going to beg for mercy?" asked the boy.

Knut and Freya laughed. "Run along, lad," said Knut.

The sing-song-voiced boy waved his stick again.

"Oh, for goodness sake!" said Freya. "Move, sunshine. We have to find my Da, Sven the Blacksmith."

"Blacksmith?" said the boy. "A Viking blacksmith?"

"That's him," said Freya. "I see his fame is well known in these parts. We're looking for him, so cheerio."

The boy ran along beside them. "Is he a big bloke with huge muscles and a leather apron?" he went on.

"Yes," replied Freya, looking suspiciously at the boy. "How do you know that?"

The boy jumped about excitedly. "I know where he is," he said.

"What?" said Freya and Knut together.

Freya leaned very close to the boy. "You tell us right now where my Da is or I'll grind your bones for the wolves."

The boy backed away. "He's the prisoner of Queen Awllbrann," he said nervously. "She's a ferocious lady who wouldn't let you come within spitting distance of her castle."

"So, how will we rescue my Da?" said Freya.

The boy tapped his head. "I have a plan," he said. "If you two pretend to be my prisoners I'll lead you right to your Da. Is it a deal?"

Knut and Freya thought for a moment. "Okay," they both said. "It's a deal."

"Oh goody," said the boy. "Now I can be Morgan the Mighty instead of Morgan the Mouse."

Chapter Five

So they set off along the valley. When they came to a patch of thick forest, Morgan suddenly began shouting.

"Move along, you miserable lot," he said at the top of his voice. "Move along or I'll grind your bones for the hounds."

"What are you playing at, you cheeky prat?" said Freya. "I'm the one who grinds bones around here."

"Sshh," said Morgan. "I'm just trying to impress the guards, you see. They're hidden up trees and behind bushes. I want them to see that I've captured you all on my own."

"Hmmppff," muttered Freya. But she didn't argue because she wanted to see her Da.

After a while they came to a castle with high walls all around it. By now the singing was really loud. Morgan the Mouse ushered Knut and Freya across a drawbridge into a cobbled courtyard. In the centre of the courtyard a group of men were singing a very long song. The castle door opened and a very large lady rushed out. She had her hands over her ears.

"Will you stop the awful noise!" she shouted. "How are we supposed to fight the Saxons when all you lot do is spend your time singing. You should be practising with swords and things. Cor, what a bunch of nerds!"

When she saw Morgan she looked very surprised. "What have you got there, Morgan the Mouse?" she asked suspiciously.

"Prisoners," replied Morgan. "Captured them myself."

"Yeah," muttered Freya. "In his dreams."

"Sshh," whispered Knut.

"Good man," said Queen Awllbrann. "They're not much to look at, but they're better than nothing. I always like to have a prisoner or two about the place."

"I'll just put them in the dungeon along with that other fellow," went on Morgan the Mouse. Looking very proud and important, he took Knut and Freya down a long flight of steps to a deep dungeon.

"Your Da should be in here somewhere," he said to Freya. "I don't come down here much myself. In fact I've never captured prisoners before."

"You didn't capture us," said Freya. "We ..."

"Sshhh, Freya," whispered Knut. "I keep telling you to keep quiet. We don't want him to change his mind and tell the queen that we've come to rescue Sven."

Knut and Freya peered into the gloomy dungeon as Morgan the Mouse held the big door open. From a far corner a strange humming sound could be heard.

"Da!" exclaimed Freya. "That's my Da, I'd know that humming anywhere. He's saying poetry."

With that she ran across the stone floor to where Sven the Blacksmith was reciting a new poem he'd learnt from his Welsh kidnappers.

"Freya!" he said as his daughter gave him a great big hug. "Have they kidnapped you too?"

"No, Da," replied Freya. "We've come to rescue you, Knut and I."

"I'm afraid that's not possible," sighed Sven.

"Why is that, Sven?" asked Knut. "Can't we just sneak out while that lot are singing and take our boat across the sea to home. We know the way."

But before Sven could answer, there was a flurry of footsteps and Queen Awllbrann stormed in.

"Well, Sven," she said. "Have you

worked it out yet?"

"Worked what out?" asked Knut.

"I've brought Sven here because he's supposed to be the best blacksmith in the world," went on the queen. "My kingdom is about to be invaded by the Saxons and my men have no helmets. They've gone all rusty and useless."

"Your men?" giggled Freya. "They certainly look rusty and useless."

"Not funny, young woman," said Queen Awllbrann. "I had hoped that Sven would make us some fine, scary-looking helmets, but ..."

"But our mine has collapsed and we have no metal," put in Morgan the Mouse.

"Well, if you have no metal, then you don't need Sven the Blacksmith," said Knut. "He only does metal stuff. So you might as well send him home."

"Not so fast, sonny," said Queen Awllbrann. "I'm desperate. That lot who are warbling outside are the only defence I have. I must have something to make them look fierce and scary. Otherwise I'll lose my lovely little kingdom." She sat down on a bundle of hay and looked very miserable.

"That's your problem, lady," said Freya. "We Vikings don't have problems like that."

Queen Awllbrann stood up and frowned at Freya very ferociously. "Well, if you Vikings are so clever, *you* come up with the answer. You can stay locked up here until you work something out that will make my men scare off the Saxons." Then she stormed out, dragging Morgan the Mouse after her. There was a loud click as the key turned.

"What will we do now, Da?" asked Freya.

Sven shrugged his big shoulders. "I don't know, honeybun," he said. "There's no metal, so how can I make scary helmets? Looks like we'll be locked up here forever. The singing is nice, though."

Knut stood up on a water-barrel and looked out through the bars of the window.

"I can see why the queen is worried," he said. "Her men have knobbly knees and they look like they've never trained as soldiers. They must spend all their time singing."

"All day, every day," said Sven. "The queen told me that they've never had to worry about being invaded. But now the Saxons are planning a mighty raid and she's going to lose everything. I wish I could help, but what can I do when there's no metal?"

"It's a pity that metal doesn't grow on trees," said Knut. "There are lots of trees all around."

At that, Freya's ears pricked up. She jumped onto the barrel beside Knut.

"You're right," she said. "Millions of trees." Then she turned to Knut. "Did you bring that chisel thing with you, Knut?"

Knut patted his belt. "I did," he said. "I never go anywhere without it. Why?"

Freya clapped her hands. "I have a brilliant idea," she said. Then she jumped from the barrel and ran to the door. "Morgan the Mouse!" she shouted at the top of her voice. "Morgan, tell the queen that we have an excellent plan!"

Chapter Six

"What do you mean, he carves bowls?" asked Queen Awllbrann. "What good are bowls against the Saxons?"

"Not bowls," said Freya. "Helmets. Knut can carve smashing wooden helmets. Same as bowls, but upside down."

"But wooden helmets wouldn't be much use, Freya," said Knut.

Freya shook her head impatiently. "These would be very special helmets, Queen," she said. "You just get your men to bring us lots of chunks of wood and we'll do the rest. On one condition."

"Oh yeah?" said Queen Awllbrann. "And what would that be?"

"My Da goes free and you give us some decent food."

"Done," said Queen Awllbrann. After all, she was pretty desperate so she'd agree to anything that might shake off those wretched Saxons.

"Get the cook to make a pile of Welsh cakes," she said to Morgan the Mouse.

And so Knut and Freya found themselves in the courtyard surrounded by a pile of Welsh cakes and big chunks of wood.

"I still don't know why you want me to carve wooden helmets, Freya," said Knut as he began carving. "Wood won't stand up against the spears and swords of the Saxons. And what are you doing with those wood-shavings?"

Freya was gathering up all the curly wood-shavings that fell away from Knut's carving.

"Just wait and see," smiled Freya.

Sven wandered off to listen to Dewi the Druid who was reciting a poem about birds and mountain streams and clouds and yellow daffs.

"This is more my kind of thing," he said. "Especially as there's no metal to hammer."

All day, and far into the night, Knut carved helmet after helmet, and Freya gathered sacks and sacks of curly wood-shavings. Every so often a Welsh person would come by and mutter about it all being a waste of time. But Freya and Knut just kept on working, and Queen Awllbrann's soldiers kept on singing.

Suddenly there was a loud clamour as a horseman rode into the

courtyard. The breathless rider dismounted and ran to where Queen Awllbrann was practising throwing big rocks in preparation for the coming battle.

"Queen Awllbrann!" cried the rider. "I've just come from the border. The Saxons are on their way here. They'll be here by morning."

"Darn," said the queen. "We haven't a hope with our wooden helmets. They're not in the least bit scary. We may as well kiss our kingdom goodbye. This is a sad moment for all of us."

The soldiers stopped singing long enough to say "Tut-tut. Shame." Then they all sang a really sad song about drizzle and fog and rotten Saxons.

"That's the last helmet," said Knut, wiping his chisel and tucking it back inside his belt.

"Yeah, thanks, sonny," said Queen Awllbrann. "Those wooden helmets should last us all of five minutes into the battle."

"We're not finished yet, Queen," said Freya. "What we need now is glue. Lots of glue."

Chapter Seven

Early the next morning Stanley the Saxon was leading his men through the valley that led to Queen Awllbrann's kingdom.

"Right, lads," he said. "I want this

kingdom. Nice scenery."

Just then forty of Queen Awllbrann's men stuck their heads over the bushes.

They were singing a song about silly Saxons. That made Stanley the Saxon very angry indeed.

"Who do they think they are, the wimps?" he said. "With their ridiculous haircuts and daft singing they haven't a hope against the might of us Saxons. And they're not even wearing helmets. Ho, ho! Put away your swords, we'll just bop them on their heads with our clubs. That'll teach them to wear protective head-gear in battle."

"*Bop,*" went the Saxons with their clubs. "*Bop, bop, bop*!"

But the more they bopped, the more the Welsh soldiers sang. The Saxon men began to grow quite nervous.

"This is really weird," said one. "They're not even wearing helmets and yet, when we bop them on the head, they just keep singing."

"This is scary," said another. "If they're so tough that they don't even need helmets, then I'm out of here."

With that all the Saxons turned and ran. Queen Awllbrann and her men cheered loudly. She hugged Knut and Freya so tight that their eyes popped.

"You wonderful Vikings!" she said.

"Well, it was mostly Freya's idea," said Knut modestly. "She's the one who thought of sticking the curly wood-shavings onto the wooden helmets to make them look like hair."

"Yes," agreed Freya. "It was a

brilliant idea. I just thought that if we could make your lads look tough and hairy, it would scare the Saxons."

"And those Saxon nellies fell for it," laughed Queen Awllbrann. "They thought we had really hard heads. It will be a long time before they come around these parts again to mess with hard-headed Welshmen. Well done!"

"Don't forget me," said Morgan the Mouse. "It was me who brought Knut and Freya here, remember."

"That's true," said Queen Awllbrann. "From now on we won't call you Morgan the Mouse. We'll call you Morgan the Mighty."

"That will do grand," said Morgan.

After a mighty feast of leek soup and Welsh cakes, it was time for Knut, Freya and Sven to sail back home. All the soldiers gathered at the shore to sing a farewell song, waving their hairy-looking wooden helmets.

Dewi the Druid gave Sven a whole bundle of poems about birds and mountain streams and clouds and yellow daffs.

"You are two heroes, Knut and Freya," said Sven proudly. "I think I could sing a Welsh song about your bravery."

"No thanks, Da," said Freya.

"Just stick with the poems and the hammering, Sven," said Knut.

The End